Tweenies™

Once Upon a Time
with four little storybooks

D1357530

One day, the Tweenies were sitting in the book corner of the playroom, sorting out a pile of little books for Judy. "I've got an idea," said Judy, suddenly. "You can all choose your favourite book and we'll make something to help us tell the story."

Jake said he wanted to read Chicken Licken because he liked animals.

So, Judy found some scraps of felt and helped the Tweenies make finger puppets. They made two each. Bella made a chicken and a hen, Milo made a cockerel and a duck, Fizz made a drake and a goose and Jake made a turkey. Then he made a furry fox finger puppet, too. The Tweenies settled down to hear the story.

"Once upon a time," Judy began, and the Tweenies used their finger puppets to help tell the story.

"It's your turn to choose
a story, Fizz," said Judy.

Fizz chose Cinderella. "I like the bit when the fairy godmother turns Cinderella's rags into a beautiful party dress," she explained.

Fizz and Bella painted a picture of sparkly shoes like the ones Cinderella wore to the ball, but Milo and Jake wanted to paint masks of the ugly sisters! Judy helped them. When they had finished, Milo decided that Doodles and Izzles would make great ugly sisters so they put the masks on them.

Judy began to tell the story.

When it came to Milo's turn, he chose The Three Billy Goats Gruff.

"I think the troll's really cool!" he said.

Milo wanted to hide under the slide and jump out and scare the other Tweenies with a nasty troll voice.

Judy helped Bella, Fizz and Jake tie some fluffy bits of fake fur around their ankles so they could be the three goats. Doodles wanted to join in, so Milo said they could both dress up as the troll. He covered Doodles with a large piece of brown material to make a cloak that left just his face peeping out.

When they were ready, Judy began to tell the story.
The Tweenies acted it out and Doodles joined in.

Next, it was Bella's turn to choose a story.

"Ooooh, let me think," said Bella, trying to remember some stories.

"I know. The story of Hansel and Gretel. That's *my* favourite story."

Bella chose Hansel and Gretel because she loved the idea of living in a house made of gingerbread and covered in sweets.

Bella wanted to make gingerbread biscuits in the shape
of houses. The Tweenies put on their overalls and Judy
helped them to make the mixture and roll it out. They
all helped to make the biscuits and Judy put them
in the oven to bake.

When the biscuits were ready, Bella said that as Doodles and Izzles had been so good they could help decorate them.

But Doodles and Izzles ate their gingerbread houses instead!

Judy began to read the story. The Tweenies sat on their beanbags, quietly munching on their gingerbread biscuits as they listened.

"I love story time," said Jake, when Judy had finished telling the story.

"Can we have another story, Judy?" asked Fizz.

"Not today, Fizz. It's getting late and we need to clear up the playroom now."

So the Tweenies put all the dressing up things back in the box and helped Judy to tidy up the messy time area. And they put all the books back on the shelf until next time.